I Talk with My Hands
The Contest

WHAT READERS ARE SAYING ...

I recommend *I Talk With My Hands: The Contest* by Jeanne Mansfield and Gail Lenhard.

As an elementary librarian for many years, I was always happy to find chapter books for the six- to ten-year-old children about students with challenges.

To read a story about a deaf child who is portrayed as leading a full life in spite of his challenge is important for children who are not challenged as well as those who are.

A book like this is important on the shelves of elementary school libraries as well as available on the book store shelves.

—Nancy S. Brett, MSLS, MSEd., school librarian, retired

I really like *I Talk With My Hands, The Contest*. I've only read the first five chapters and can't wait to read the rest. The signing is cool. I want to know what is wrong with Nathan and find out if Danny's birdhouse wins the contest. This is a great book.

—William, age 9

I Talk with My Hands
The Contest

Jeanne Mansfield
and
Gail Lenhard

ELK LAKE PUBLISHING INC
PUBLISHING THE POSITIVE
Plymouth, Massachusetts

COPYRIGHT NOTICE

Cover Design: Jeff Gilbert, Derinda Babcock

Interior Design: Derinda Babcock

Editor(s): Linda Farmer Harris, Deb Haggerty

Author Represented By:

PUBLISHED BY: Elk Lake Publishing, Inc., 35 Dogwood Drive, Plymouth, MA 02360, 2022

Library Cataloging Data

Names: Mansfield, Jeanne and Lenhard, Gail (Jeanne Mansfield and Gail Lenhard)

I Talk with My Hands: The Contest / Jeanne Mansfield and Gail Lenhard

70 p. 23cm × 15cm (9in × 6 in.)

ISBN-13: 978-1-64949-489-4 (paperback) | 978-1-64949-490-0 (trade paperback) | 978-1-64949-491-7 (e-book)

Key Words: Children's books, Ages 6-10; Deaf; family relationships; bullying; problem-solving; disabilities & special needs; siblings

Library of Congress Control Number: 2022931009 Fiction

DEDICATION

Jeanne
To Gail, for saying yes.

Gail
To my mom, who showed me she could still do anything
she wanted to, even though she was deaf.

CONTENTS

**Kindness is the language
the blind can see and the deaf can hear.**
Taken from a quote by Christian Nestell Bovee 1857

CHAPTER 1: THE RED BIKE

Danny Greene grabbed his dad's arm and pointed to the two bright red bicycles on display in the craft store window. He made a pedaling motion with his hands then signed, "I want a bike."

A poster leaned against the front tires.

BARTLETT'S CRAFT STORE
ANNUAL KIDS' CRAFT
CONTEST
Date: July 29
Two Age Groups
5-7 year olds
8-11 year olds
PRIZES ... PRIZES ... PRIZES
Entry forms inside store

Dad frowned and signed, "Mom worries—."

"I know ... because I'm deaf. I promise I'll be careful." He shifted from one foot to the other, waiting for his dad's response. "I'm almost nine. Can I enter?"

"We'll see."

"What about Mom?"

Dad winked. "I'll talk to your mother. You could enter one of your birdhouses."

"Yes." Danny pumped his fist.

When Bartlett's door slid open, Danny stopped, awed by the size of the store. *Wow. Cool.* The spicy smell of dried floral materials reminded him of the craft store in Denver.

Danny signed to his father, "I need paint."

"I need cabinet knobs," Dad signed.

Danny took a cart and followed the overhead arrows. Near the back of the store, he saw a boy about his age and a man waving his arms. *Oh, oh. Somebody is in trouble.* He hurried on to the paint aisle.

The paint section had every color imaginable.

He closed his eyes and tried to remember what paints he had in his new workshop. *Need yellow and blue.*

Something struck his shoulder.

Hard.

Danny clutched the cart to keep from falling. He spun around and faced the same boy he had just seen. "Hey!"

The boy glared. A dirty baseball cap sat backward on his head, dark brown hair hung over his eyes. Paint stained his Bartlett's Craft Store apron.

Danny recognized the word "move" from his lipreading classes. Before he could respond, the boy shoved him. He stumbled backwards into a display.

Cans of paint and brushes tumbled to the floor.

Danny jumped up and shoved the boy, who flapped his arms to keep from falling.

Eyes glaring, they faced each other.

The boy backed away.

Danny turned to see the same man he had seen with the boy earlier.

The man yanked the boy to the side of the aisle.

Danny watched their facial expressions and body language. He could tell the man was very angry.

The boy's face turned red.

Danny made out the words. "Busy ... work ... now."

The boy sneered, hitched up his jeans, and swaggered away.

Danny rubbed his shoulder and looked at the man. "Are you hurt?"

Danny held up a finger and pulled out his cell phone.

DANNY: I'm deaf. Who was that kid?

The man fumbled in his apron pocket for a notepad and pencil.

MAN: My son, Nathan. I'm Mr. Bartlett, the owner. Are you okay?

DANNY: I'm okay.

MR. BARTLETT: You sure?

DANNY: Yes.

After Mr. Bartlett put the displays back in order, he faced Danny. He gestured to the front of the store.

Danny turned and saw a customer waiting.

Mr. Bartlett hurried away.

Danny's dad walked up and placed the knobs in the cart. "Everything okay?"

"Yes."

Dad rubbed his chin like he wanted to say something, but Danny turned to the paint shelves. *I can take care of myself.* He focused on the display, then reached for a can of Cherry Red. *Red like the bike.*

Dad held up Ocean Blue.

Danny made a thumbs up sign. He found two more colors he wanted, Canary Yellow and Dove White, and added them to the cart.

Dad handed him two large tubes of fast-drying wood glue and a package of different sized paintbrushes. "Ready?"

When they went to check out, Danny scanned the aisles for Nathan. *Bet he's in big trouble now.*

They paid and left.

They put the supplies in the trunk of their car.

Dad handed Danny the sales flyer announcing the Grand Opening of Emmerson's Lumber Yard. "Next stop."

Danny got in the car and leaned against the window. *Nathan. What a jerk. Are kids in Nashville like him?*

CHAPTER 2: COLORADO FRIEND

When the door to Emmerson's opened, Danny inhaled the sharp scent of cedar and pine. He loved the smell of wood.

They found and selected shelves for the home office and a new saw for Danny to replace the one he broke.

They spotted a sign offering free Odds and Ends.

Danny selected several pieces of wood. *These are perfect for birdhouses.*

Dad touched his watch. "Need to hurry. Mom's waiting."

After dinner, Mom brought out the sign language card game, Fingerspell Flash. She separated the manual alphabet cards from the sign language cards. Starting with the alphabet, she held up a card, and they took turns signing the letter.

Six-year-old JoJo pulled her middle finger over her index finger, trying to form the letter R. She struggled with some of the other letters but had no problem signing the letter J.

Danny laughed when his dad confused the letters G and Q and ducked when his dad threw a sofa pillow at him.

Everyone practiced fingerspelling the pictures shown on the sign language cards.

Mom turned to Danny and signed, "Want to try some lipreading?"

"Yes," he said aloud.

Mom said a word slowly.

Danny signed, "Shower."

Mom smiled. She continued saying words for him.

Dad signed, "Good job."

Danny couldn't sleep. He thought about the jerk at the craft store and punched his pillow. He blew out a breath to calm himself. *What is his problem?*

He wanted to talk to someone about Nathan and thought of Charlie, his good friend in Colorado. He smiled, remembering the pranks they pulled in their speech classes at the school for the deaf. Charlie had given him the name sign D-Bird because he always built birdhouses.

He checked the time on his nightstand clock and decided to text his friend.

DANNY: Hi, Charlie.

CHARLIE: Hey, D-Bird, what's up?

DANNY: Bad day.

CHARLIE: What happened?

DANNY: Went to craft store for paint. Owner's son pushed me.

CHARLIE: No way. Why?

DANNY: He's a bully like Larry from our sign language class.

CHARLIE: Wow. What'd you do?

DANNY: Shoved him back.

CHARLIE: Good for you.

DANNY: Thanks.

CHARLIE: How's your new place?

DANNY: Got a real cool workshop.

CHARLIE: Better than basement in old house?

DANNY: Lots. Windows, big workbench. Hung the hockey poster of Wayne Gretzky you gave me.

CHARLIE: Cool. Predators fan now?

DANNY: Don't know, maybe.

CHARLIE: Start speech class?

DANNY: No. Working on lipreading.

CHARLIE: Not easy.

DANNY: True, but kinda fun.

Danny told Charlie about the store's contest and the red bike. His bad mood lifted as they texted back and forth.

Charlie ended the call with a "fingers crossed" emoji and Win bike. Good luck.

Danny sent the "thumbs up" and "wave" emojis.

He put the phone back on the charger, turned off the lamp, and drifted off to sleep.

The next morning, while his dad watched, Danny practiced cutting pieces of wood with his new saw. The woodsy scent reminded him of a Christmas tree farm.

"Good job. Be careful, blade is sharp." Dad patted his son's back and left.

Feeling a vibration through the wooden floor, Danny turned to see his sister, JoJo, at the door.

She twirled her strawberry blond pigtails. "Come in?"

Danny pulled the stool out from under the workbench.

JoJo plopped down, looked at the instructions, and signed, "Birdhouse?"

"Want to help?" Danny picked up his saw and cut a piece of wood.

Fine sawdust filled the air, making JoJo sneeze three times. She wiped her nose on her sleeve.

He handed her two pieces of wood.

She held them steady while he glued them together.

They worked all afternoon. When the last piece was in place, they stood back to admire their work.

He put the sign for C on his right temple and a backward L on his left. His eyes formed the double Os. "Cool."

JoJo laughed and tried to copy her brother's silly sign. She gave up and rubbed her stomach. "I'm hungry."

"Me too."

"Mom's calling me."

Danny started to put his tools away. He looked out the big back window in time to see a black bike coming down the alley. Bright red racing stripes were painted on the frame.

The rider wasn't wearing a helmet, instead he wore a backwards baseball cap.

The hair on Danny's neck stood on end. *Nathan? Does he know where I live?*

He double-checked the window latches before he locked the workshop door. He gave the lock one more tug, just to be sure.

CHAPTER 3: BEDLAM

Danny helped his dad hang the shelves in the office.

Mom watched from the doorway. When they finished, she signed, "Thank you for letting your sister help you. She had fun."

"Me too." He stifled a yawn.

Dad touched his watch. "Bedtime."

Danny yawned again, hugged his mom and dad good night, and went upstairs.

The next morning, Danny and JoJo raced across the backyard to his workshop.

They painted the birdhouse walls yellow and the roof blue.

JoJo added flowers and leaves around the opening. When she stood to admire her work, she dropped the paintbrush on the floor. Paint splattered all over her jeans.

Danny laughed at her surprised expression. He picked up the brush and handed her a towel to wipe up the paint.

JoJo held the door open so her brother could carry the freshly painted birdhouse outside. They crossed the lawn to the patio by the backdoor. Danny set the birdhouse on the picnic table.

JoJo bounced up and down. "Pretty. Show friend." She made the letter X with her index fingers then hooked her right finger over the left then reversed them.

Movement by the chain-linked fence caught Danny's attention.

The gate opened.

A young girl with dark brown hair walked into the yard. She wore a bright orange tee shirt with a huge number 6 on the front.

A boy followed her.

Nathan.

Danny froze, his eyes narrowed. *Why is he here?*

JoJo ran to the gate, took her friend's hand, and they skipped to the picnic table.

Danny clapped to get his sister's attention. He gestured with his thumb at Nathan, who walked around the yard kicking the grass.

JoJo held up her finger. She looked at Chloe, said and signed, "Your brother?"

Chloe nodded.

The two girls sat on the bench and ignored the boys.

Danny watched Nathan pick up and throw a small, thick branch.

The branch knocked the birdhouse off the table, startling the girls.

Nathan walked over and poked his finger on Danny's chest. "My dad said you're deaf. Are you stupid, too?"

Danny pushed Nathan away. "Stop!" He turned when JoJo grabbed his arm.

"Danny is deaf, and he's way smarter than you." She clenched her fists.

Nathan started toward JoJo.

Danny stepped in front of his sister. "No. Go. Now."

"Make me." The boy looked at Danny, arms crossed, eyes two slits like a snake.

Danny stood his ground.

Chloe pulled her brother's arm.

Nathan shook her off. He picked up and smashed the birdhouse to the ground. Pieces went flying. He took off across the lawn, slamming the gate behind him.

Stunned, JoJo and Chloe looked at Danny with tears running down their faces.

Danny looked at the broken birdhouse, too shocked to react.

The girls began to gather the pieces.

He picked up what was left.

CHAPTER 4: DANNY'S DILEMMA

Danny followed the girls into the workshop.

They set the pieces on the workbench and carefully fitted them together like a puzzle.

Once the glue had dried, Danny opened the cans of paint, stirred each one, and handed the girls a paintbrush. *Good thing not contest birdhouse.*

He watched them paint, ducking when JoJo rinsed her paintbrush and flipped water everywhere.

Danny felt a strong vibration through the floor and turned to see Mom.

She burst out laughing seeing the girls covered with paint, tapped her watch, and motioned to the house.

The girls put the brushes in the water jar and ran out of the workshop.

Danny sighed.

Mom tapped his arm. "Hey, D-Bird, something wrong?" She often used his nickname. She touched her forehead with the sign for *D*, then formed the closed letter *L* in front of her mouth, fingers pointing outward, opened and closed her fingers several times like a bird's beak.

Danny shook his head.

"You sure?"

Danny signed, "Chloe's brother smashed birdhouse."

"Why?

"He's a bully."

"I'm going to call his mother right now." She started toward the door.

Danny tugged her arm, shook his head, and said, "No."

She turned back to him, "No?"

"No."

"We will discuss this later." She blew him a kiss and left.

Danny knew his mom wasn't happy. He didn't want her to interfere. *Nathan is my problem.* He started to clean the girls' mess and knocked over a can of paint.

Blue paint dripped to the floor.

He twisted the cap back on the can, grabbed a dirty towel, and mopped up the paint. Danny plopped down on the stool and stared at the birdhouse.

Completely lost in thought, he jumped when JoJo stomped on the workshop floor.

She signed eating.

He closed the workshop door, double checked the lock, and followed JoJo to the house.

His mom had made one of his favorites, spaghetti and meatballs. He didn't feel like eating.

He twirled the noodles around his plate and watched JoJo's mouth. He understood a few words, "Chloe," "Nathan," "birdhouse," "paint," but she talked too fast.

Mom put her fork down. "Mrs. Bartlett called me when Chloe told her what happened. Nathan's dad will speak to him."

Dad touched his son's arm. "Boy from store?"

"Yeah." Danny looked down at his plate. *Great. Another reason for Nathan to hate me.* After eating a few bites, he patted the table, put a finger on his chest, then looked toward the ceiling.

Mom signed, "Okay."

Danny took his dishes to the kitchen, ran up to his room, and flopped on his bed. Tears stung his eyes. *Wish we could go back to Denver.*

CHAPTER 5: H-O-R-S-E

Danny groaned and pushed back the covers to see JoJo standing at the foot of his bed.

"Get up. Leaving." She tugged on his big toe.

Danny pulled the covers over his head.

She yanked the blankets onto the floor and ran from the room.

He got up and threw them back on the bed. He tossed his pajamas on the chair, grabbed his jeans and shirt, dressed, and hurried downstairs.

Danny found everyone in the living room. He held up his index finger and rocked his hand side to side. "Where?"

"Park. Picnic. H-O-R-S-E. Remember rules?" Dad signed.

JoJo practically jumped out of her chair. "I do, I do."

Danny remembered he had lost the last game he played when he didn't copy Charlie's moves, missed the basket, and spelled the word H-O-R-S-E first.

JoJo raised her hand. "Can Chloe come?"

Mom shook her head. "Not this time."

Danny hid a grin. *No Nathan.*

Danny dribbled the basketball on the sidewalk, waiting for his parents.

A shiny black bicycle zoomed by him.

Danny barely had time to leap out of the way to avoid being hit. *Nathan.* He watched the bike careen around the corner. *He almost hit me. Wish I could hear.*

Dad walked out of the garage. He pulled a wagon loaded with picnic gear.

Mom came out of the house and locked the door.

Danny trailed behind his parents, basketball tucked under his arm. He took one more look around for the black bike, then raced to catch up with the others.

JoJo stood at the intersection, turned to her family, and stomped her foot. She formed two Hs with her hands and shook them up and down. "Hurry."

When everyone reached the corner, JoJo took Danny's hand, pulling him across the street and into the park.

They sprinted to claim an empty table under the pavilion.

"Good spot." Mom unfolded the tablecloth and covered the picnic table.

Dad nudged Danny, putting his finger to his lips. He reached into the cooler and snatched a handful of ice. "JoJo, catch."

JoJo shrieked and ran.

Danny and his father roared with laughter.

Mom shook her finger and ducked as a handful of ice flew by.

JoJo poked her brother's arm. She put her thumb against the side of her head, bent her two fingers twice, and signed, "Horse."

Mom signed, "Wait for Dad."

The three of them walked around the little lake to the basketball court.

Two kids were already playing.

JoJo nudged Danny. "Horse?"

The boy missed a shot, and the basketball rolled toward Danny, who stopped the ball with his foot.

"I'll be back when lunch is ready." Dad left.

The boy came over.

Danny watched his sister talk to the boy and girl.

"Hi. I'm JoJo. He's my brother, Danny. He's almost nine. He can't hear. He was born deaf."

The girl looked at Danny. "Can he talk?"

"He talks with his hands."

The boy's eyes widened. "Show me."

Danny had no problems reading his lips. He gave his basketball to JoJo and pulled out his cell phone.

> **DANNY**: names?

He handed his phone to the boy.

> **LIAM:** Liam, she's Lili. We live across the street in the yellow house with the red door.

Lili took the phone.

> **LILI:** We're twins. He's tallest. I'm oldest. We're ten.

JoJo looked at the twins. "You don't look alike."

Liam took the phone.

> **LIAM:** We hear this a lot. How do you talk with your hands?

Danny showed them how to fingerspell their names.

Tired of waiting, JoJo waved her hand in front of her brother's face and dribbled the ball down the court. She stood under the basket and threw the ball straight up.

SWOOSH!

Lili followed JoJo's actions. Standing under the basket, she tossed the ball, which bounced off the backboard.

"She's got the *H*," JoJo said and signed.

They copied each other's silly movements until someone missed enough shots to spell the word H-O-R-S-E.

They laughed when Danny showed them how to do the "cool sign" using their eyes as Os.

Soon, they were using the few signs Danny taught them, "Nice shot" — "Cool" — "My turn."

The basketball slipped from Danny's hands when Nathan stepped out from behind the bushes by the fence. *What's he doing here?*

Nathan swaggered onto the court. He reached for the basketball JoJo had picked up and held close to her chest.

"Go," Danny said aloud. He moved in front of his sister.

Nathan laughed. He pushed Danny aside and slapped the ball from JoJo's hands. He ran to the fence and took off down the street on his bike.

JoJo raced to retrieve the ball.

Danny blew out the breath he had been holding. He reached for his phone.

DANNY: You know him?

LIAM: He's a punk. Ignore him.

DANNY: What's his problem?

LIAM: Who knows? Let's play.

CHAPTER 6: RESCUED

JoJo held her hand up to stop the game. "Lunch time."

They told their new friends goodbye and walked toward their dad, who waited nearby.

JoJo stopped, held up her finger, and looked back at Liam and Lili.

When she turned back around, Danny shrugged his shoulders and raised his hands, palms up.

"They want to learn how to talk with their hands."

Danny smiled. *I like doing something other kids can't do.*

On their way back to the pavilion, the thought of Nathan made Danny look around. *I'm not afraid of him.*

Mom had set the table with crispy fried chicken, a bowl of potato salad, sliced watermelon, and cookies.

Danny sat beside JoJo and reached for a drumstick. A hand stopped him. He looked up to see his mother shaking her head.

"Wash." Mom pretended to wash her hands. She touched JoJo's arm. "You, too."

Danny got a kick out of watching his sister talk about Liam and Lili. Most of the time she talked too fast for him to keep up, but he didn't mind. He took another cookie.

He watched a little squirrel stand on his hind legs, begging. He tossed a piece of cookie and laughed when the animal caught the morsel and ran up the nearby tree.

Dad sat down across from Danny and waved his hand. "Don't feed the squirrels. They get lazy."

His exaggerated signing and silly facial expressions made everyone laugh.

Danny tapped the table and pointed to the darkening sky.

They quickly cleaned the area and packed the wagon.

Just as they arrived home, rain poured from the huge black clouds.

Danny and JoJo stood by the window and watched the river of water flowing down the street.

Danny jumped.

JoJo looked at him. "Did you hear the thunder?"

"No, house shook."

"Yes, it did." JoJo clapped her hands over her ears. "Loud, too. Can I play a game on your phone?"

Danny handed her his phone.

She walked away, tapping on the phone.

The rain hit the window sideways. Danny liked watching thunderstorms.

Lightning streaked across the sky.

"Dog!"

JoJo ran to the window.

Danny jerked open the front door. He started slapping his leg trying to coax the trembling animal out of the storm.

The dog refused to budge and cowered by the bottom steps.

A huge flash of lightning lit the sky.

The dog flew past Danny into the house. He slid to a stop and shook, spraying water everywhere.

JoJo jumped back, covering her face with her hands.

Mom handed Danny a towel.

He dried the tan and white dog. "No collar."

The dog walked over to JoJo and licked her hand. She giggled and rubbed his head. "Lucky you saw him."

"Lucky. Good name." Danny gave his sister a thumbs-up. "Mom, what kind of dog is he?"

"He looks like a Sheltie."

"Keep him?" Danny looked at his parents.

"We need to find his owner." Dad walked into the office.

CHAPTER 7: LUCKY

Danny looked over his father's shoulder as he scrolled through the SPCA's LOST DOGS section of the website.

None of the photos matched.

Dad typed in the information requested under FOUND DOGS, adding a picture Danny took with his cell phone.

Danny and JoJo exchanged worried looks.

"Any luck?" Mom walked into the office.

Dad shook his head.

Mom leaned over and massaged Lucky's ears. "Microchipped?"

"Good idea. I'll check in the morning."

JoJo pulled Danny's shirt. She rubbed her tummy. "Lucky's hungry."

In the kitchen, Mom cracked three eggs into a bowl and handed Danny a fork. While he scrambled them, his mom grated cheddar cheese. He poured the mixture into the pan and stirred.

Mom nudged him.

He turned to see JoJo on the floor beside Lucky. Both sound asleep.

The next morning, Dad found a website for Dr. Hoffman, a veterinarian who had an office close by.

The vet agreed to check the dog for a microchip.

Danny patted his leg. "Come."

The dog followed him to the garage and jumped into the car, his big fluffy tail wagging.

Doctor Hoffman walked out of the examination room shaking his head.

"No chip, but the dog is healthy," Dad said and signed. He shook the vet's hand.

Back in the car, Mom faced the back seat. "Don't get your hopes up.

Dad pulled the car close to the grocery store's automatic doors to keep Mom out of the rain.

She dashed inside. Soon she was back under the awning, waving.

After she got into the car, she turned and faced the kids. "I bought food, treats, a collar, and a leash."

Danny nudged JoJo.

CHAPTER 8: ANOTHER ENCOUNTER

Dad switched the wipers to their fastest setting and headed for home.

A bright streak of lightning made Lucky jump.

Danny stroked the trembling dog.

By the time they arrived home, the rain had slowed to a light drizzle.

Dad pushed the remote to open the garage door and drove inside. He turned to Danny and JoJo, "Take Lucky outside."

JoJo scowled. "Outside? Lucky hates rain."

"Potty." Mom formed the letter *T*, her palm facing forward, and shook her fist from side to side.

Danny put the new collar and leash on Lucky. "Come." He coaxed the dog outside.

After a short time, Lucky raced back into the garage, pulling Danny behind him.

JoJo tried to dry the wiggling dog with an old towel.

Mom opened the kitchen door and jumped out of the way as Lucky raced inside, sliding to a stop at the dish of food on the floor.

Danny laughed. *He's hungry.*

The storms continued over the next few days.

Between downpours, Danny ran to his workshop. He drew several birdhouse designs, but none were quite right for the contest.

JoJo tagged along. She practiced painting flowers on an old piece of cardboard.

Lucky laid on his bed near the workshop door.

JoJo pounded on the table.

Danny looked up and saw Lucky jumping against the door. He pulled the door open just as Nathan bolted over the fence. *Is he spying on me?*

"Good dog." Danny patted Lucky's head.

"Tell Mom?"

Danny shook his head.

JoJo frowned and signed, "Okay. I won't."

Danny checked the windows and locked the door. He wasn't taking any chances with Nathan lurking around.

The next morning, the bright sun in the blue cloudless sky made everything sparkle.

Danny nudged his sister and looked up at the two birds perched on the repaired blue and yellow birdhouse their dad had hung in the tree. "Birds found house."

A house wren perched on the roof, another peeked out of the opening.

Danny made the sign for baby birds.

JoJo danced around signing, "Yes, yes, yes."

Lucky ran around the backyard. He started digging a hole in the flowerbed while Mom pulled weeds. She shooed him away.

JoJo pulled Danny's sleeve. They ran to the chain-linked fence.

Mrs. Tinkham handed a plate of cookies to Danny. "New dog?"

Mom walked to the fence, brushing dirt from her gloves. "No, Cora, he's lost. We're looking for his owner," Mom said and signed.

Danny stuffed another cookie in his mouth.

"Dinner soon." Mom took the plate of cookies. She thanked their neighbor and went into the house.

Mrs. Tinkham looked up and nodded toward the tree. "Pretty birdhouse."

JoJo pointed to her brother. "He built. I painted flowers."

"Build one for me?" Mrs. Tinkham pulled on her bright pink apron. "Pink with flowers?"

"Yes," Danny and JoJo said at the same time.

"Thank you." The neighbor waved and went into her house.

Danny and JoJo high-fived each other.

JoJo turned to her brother. "Mom wants me." She and Lucky went inside.

Danny headed to his workshop but stopped short. The hairs on his neck bristled. A black bike leaned against the neighbor's wooden fence across the alley. *Nathan.* He looked around but didn't see anyone.

Just then, Nathan stepped out from behind the dumpster. Making a V with his fingers, he aimed them at his own eyes then at Danny.

Without hesitation, Danny made the same sign right back.

Nathan sneered, jumped on his bike, and took off down the alley.

CHAPTER 9: BUTTERFLIES AND BIRDHOUSES

"Dad?" Danny waited for his dad to put the newspaper down.

"Need paint. Neighbor wants birdhouse."

"Okay. Tomorrow?"

"Cool."

JoJo and Lucky walked into the living room. "What's cool?" She sat on the rug next to the dog, scratching behind his ears.

"Getting paint tomorrow."

"Me too? Me too?"

Danny made a small circle near his forehead with his index finger pretending to think about JoJo's request. Laughing, he gave her the okay sign.

Danny never tired of the fresh-cut wood aroma when the doors swished opened at Emmerson's. He headed straight to the free Odds and Ends pile and picked out pieces of wood for his neighbor's birdhouse.

Back in the car, JoJo signed and talked non-stop.

Danny noticed her signing had improved, but he was relieved when they arrived at Bartlett's. *JoJo talks too much.*

Danny stopped and gazed at the bikes. *I hope I win.*

JoJo jumped up and down and pointed to the poster. "Can I? Can I?"

Dad shrugged. "Okay. What will you make?"

"Butterflies." She pranced around pretending to fly.

Danny rolled his eyes. He pointed to the sign on the door.

STORE CLOSING FOR INVENTORY AT NOON TODAY

They had thirty minutes.

Hurrying inside, Danny watched his dad and JoJo head off to get the supplies she needed for her butterflies. He ran to the paint aisle.

At the end of the aisle, Danny saw two boys checking out the spray paint case. He watched them out of the corner of his eye. One of them held a screwdriver. *What are they up to*?

When the screwdriver fell to the floor, the boys looked around.

Danny saw the screwdriver fall, but didn't react. Instead, he held up two small paint cans and pretended to read the labels so he could see the boys' mouths.

"Hurry. He's not paying any attention to us." They fumbled with the lock again, opened the display, and stuffed several cans of spray paint into their backpacks.

Danny put the two cans of paint on the shelf, snatched a can of bright Bubble Gum pink paint, and went to find his dad.

His dad and JoJo stood at the checkout counter with Mr. Bartlett.

Danny set the can of paint on the counter, grabbed his dad's arm, and signed, "Two boys. Screwdriver. Steal spray paint."

Dad told Mr. Bartlett who hurried away.

A few minutes later, he returned, and shook Danny's hand. "Thank you. I caught them with the spray paint in their backpack. They're being detained in my office."

Dad signed what Mr. Bartlett said, and added, "You stopped a robbery."

I stopped a robbery?

Mr. Bartlett shook his head when Danny's dad tried to pay. "No charge. Thanks again."

Danny followed his dad and JoJo to the front door.

Nathan, coming in the door, brushed against Danny and mouthed, "Loser."

Danny stuck his tongue out at Nathan.

CHAPTER 10: LIPREADING CLASS

Danny laughed as Lucky ran in a circle around JoJo.

Mom came out of the office, hands covering her ears. "What's going on?"

Danny, reading his mother's lips, shrugged, and looked at his sister.

"I'm going to make butterflies for the contest. Danny stopped two boys from stealing at the store. We didn't have to pay."

Dad explained what happened at the craft store.

Danny blushed when his mom gave him a hug and kissed his cheek.

JoJo showed her mom the clothespins and colorful pipe cleaners.

"Computer." Danny took his sister's hand and pulled her into the office.

He sat at the computer and Googled directions for making butterfly wings and printed the instructions. He checked the SPCA's website. No new LOST DOG postings. He made a thumbs up sign.

When Danny came downstairs the next morning, he saw his mom putting a notebook and flashcards in a tote bag. He groaned. *Speech therapy.*

"Today?" He flopped on the couch.

Mom tapped her watch before heading into the kitchen. "Fifteen minutes."

Danny took his cell phone out, entered his password, and opened the *Baseball 9* game app.

JoJo sat next to him with Lucky by her feet and watched her brother navigate the game.

Mom motioned to Danny. "Go now."

He stopped the game and shoved his phone in his pocket.

Lucky followed them to the garage door, tail wagging.

Mom held her hand out. "No, Lucky. Sit."

The dog obeyed.

JoJo stroked the dog's silky fur.

Dad entered the kitchen and tousled Danny's hair. "Have fun." He went to the counter and poured a cup of coffee.

Danny sighed and stomped to the garage.

When his mom parked the car, Danny looked up from his game. Instead of an office building with lots of glass windows, like his old therapy office, he saw a yellow house with purple shutters and a bright green door.

The sign on the door read:

SPEECH-LANGUAGE THERAPY
JULIE PERRY, SPEECH-LANGUAGE PATHOLOGIST

Inside the house, colorful posters showing familiar words in American Sign Language hung on the walls. Several hand-held mirrors, flashcards, notepads, pencils, and crayons were arranged on the table.

A tall middle-aged woman greeted Danny's mom.

She turned to him and spoke, "Hi, Danny. Nice to meet you. I'm Mrs. Perry." She formed a P with her right hand, touched her chin, then her chest.

Danny copied her name sign and said, "Hi." He showed her his name sign—D-Bird.

The therapist motioned for them to sit at the table. She sat across from Danny and kept her face still as she enunciated each word. "How are you?"

"Good."

"We are going to work on lipreading."

Danny took the poster she gave him showing lip shapes. Several shapes had more than one letter beneath them.

While the therapist worked with Danny on lipreading skills, Danny's mom took notes.

He sighed and fidgeted. "This is hard."

"Yes, but you are doing great." After she spoke, she signed her response.

The compliment made Danny sit up straighter.

"Practice every day?"

"No. Most days."

"The more you practice, the more you will understand. Mrs. Perry said and signed.

Danny grimaced.

Mom said without signing, "Pay attention, D-Bird."

Danny nodded.

Mrs. Perry touched his arm. "Did you lipread your mother?"

"Yes."

Mrs. Perry used Danny's picture flashcards and had him show her the ASL sign for the picture on the card, then say the word aloud.

He got through nine cards before he goofed up.

"Good job." The therapist stood.

"We use the flashcards for game night," Mom said and signed.

"Good idea. Enough work for today, Danny." She paused a moment. "See you next week. Keep practicing."

Danny signed, "I will."

Back in the car, Mom turned to Danny. "Ice cream?"

"DQ?"

Mom gave him a thumbs-up.

CHAPTER 11: CONTEST BIRDHOUSE

He went to his workshop and rummaged through the box of wood scraps, finding part of a picket fence. He turned the piece over in his hands. *This looks like a church steeple. A church birdhouse?* He pumped his fist in the air. "Yes."

On his sketch pad he drew a basic birdhouse. He jotted other ideas down ... a steeple with an actual bell, red doors with an opening for the birds, painted stained-glass windows, bushes, and flowers. He thought about what colors he would need.

He checked his supplies. *Hmmm. Just need a bell and stained-glass windows? I have everything else.* He measured his wood pieces and cut them into the shapes needed.

Danny worked for days in secret. He allowed no one to come into the workshop. He taped cardboard on the window, then he covered the birdhouse with a sheet when he left.

He found his mom in the kitchen. "Can I look at the Christmas ornaments?"

She motioned for him to follow her to the garage. She pulled a box marked "Christmas" from the shelf.

"Put the box back when you are finished." Mom walked back into the house.

He rummaged through the ornaments and found a bell for the steeple. *Perfect.* He discovered a smaller box with a couple of stained-glass ornaments shaped like church windows.

They were flat, not round and reminded him of the stained-glass windows at his old church. One depicted several angels, the other ornament had stars.

He held one of them to the light and noticed some of the paint had to be retouched.

Danny looked up to see Mom.

She glanced at the ornaments scattered around the floor and put her hands on her hips.

"I'll clean up, Mom." Danny held up the two ornaments and the bell, eyes pleading.

Mom smiled. "Okay." She waved her hand at the mess then walked back into the house.

Danny carefully repacked the ornaments and put the box back on the shelf. He raced to the workshop and hung the bell in the steeple—*a perfect fit*. He touched up the paint on the stained-glass window ornaments and glued them on the birdhouse. They stood out against the pale-yellow church structure.

The day of the contest finally arrived.

Danny and JoJo hurried through breakfast, too excited to eat much.

Dad helped Danny carry the sheet-covered birdhouse to the car.

JoJo put her box of colorful butterflies in the trunk and scrambled into the car.

Both Danny and JoJo fidgeted in the back seat.

At the store, Dad helped Danny place the birdhouse in a cart.

Mom held the box of butterflies while JoJo got out of the car.

Inside the store an area had been cleared and tables set up to display the entries.

Danny watched his mom and sister take the butterflies to the tables marked AGE GROUP FIVE TO SEVEN.

With his dad's help, Danny set his church birdhouse on the table marked AGE GROUP EIGHT TO ELEVEN. He checked to make sure everything was perfect.

JoJo touched her brother's arm, pointing to Liam and Lili.

They went to see the clever pirate ship Liam had made from egg cartons.

"Wow." Danny made the sign for W with both hands, put one on each cheek, and opened his mouth to form the letter O.

They laughed as they copied Danny's wow.

The other entries in the eight to eleven age category included a cute dog hotel, a seashell wind chime, another birdhouse in the shape of a boot, beaded flowers in a vase, and a woven basket.

Danny pointed to Lili's dream catcher and signed, "Pretty."

The four kids walked over to the younger age group's table and found JoJo's four butterflies next to three colorful candle holders made from potato chip cans, a painted pet rock family, a popsicle stick house, handmade pinwheels, and an angel made from a paper towel roll.

Spotting his mom, Danny and JoJo said goodbye to their friends and walked over to stand with their parents.

Two judges entered and began walking around the tables, pausing by each entry, and taking notes.

Danny squirmed. He scratched his head, checked the time on his phone, stuffed his hands into his pockets, and pulled them back out.

Mom patted Danny on the shoulder.

"Wiggle worm," Dad joked.

A brief time later, Mr. Bartlett tested the microphone.

Mom stood where Danny could see her sign and see Mr. Bartlett at the same time.

Mr. Bartlett welcomed everyone. "Thank you all for coming. We have many beautiful entries this year among the two groups. The judges have made their decisions. Time to announce the winners of the five to seven age group."

"Honorable Mention goes to Lori Edwards for her imaginative paper towel roll angel."

Danny clapped and watched a young redheaded girl walk over to the lectern to receive her light-blue ribbon.

"Third prize and a Dairy Queen gift certificate goes to JoJo Greene for her colorful clothespin butterflies."

Danny watched his sister jump up and down, her hand clasped over her mouth, eyes wide.

JoJo ran to the front to get her prize. She raced back holding her white ribbon and gift certificate. "Look. Look. I won. I won."

Mom and Dad gave her a hug.

Danny high-fived her.

"Second prize and a certificate for a pizza party for eight goes to Nancy Callahan for her creative candle holders."

Danny watched the girl race to the front to receive her red ribbon and certificate.

Nathan wheeled the smaller bicycle out to the podium. "First prize for this age group, and this wonderful bike, goes to Phillip Young for his artistic pet rock family."

Danny watched a red-faced, dark-haired boy run to the front, grinning from ear to ear. He held his blue ribbon and stood next to the bike. Someone snapped a picture.

Mr. Bartlett held up his hand.

Danny could barely stand still. He watched his mom's hands.

"And in the next age category ... Honorable Mention goes to Jamie Boswell for her beautiful seashell wind chimes."

Danny watched a girl get her light blue ribbon. He ran his hands through his hair and looked at his mom.

"Third Place and a book of coupons for the Mall Cinema go to Andrew Quinn for his unique dog hotel."

Danny rubbed his sweaty palms up and down his jeans and watched Andrew run to the front to get his white ribbon and prize.

Mom patted his back.

"Second Place, and a certificate for a pizza party for eight, goes to Liam Knight for his very clever pirate ship."

Liam's face beamed as he walked up to get his red ribbon and certificate.

Danny signed, "Liam loves pizza."

His eyes grew wide when Nathan wheeled out the bicycle for the 8-11 age group. He looked at his mom.

"And last, but not least, the winner of this beautiful bike goes to..."

Danny squeezed his eyes shut and held his breath. *Please, please, please...*

CHAPTER 12: AND THE WINNER IS...

JoJo tugged her brother's shirt.

Danny opened his eyes. "What?"

"You won! You won!" She jumped up and down.

"I won?" He looked at his mom who gestured to the lectern.

Dad gave him a quick hug and a little shove to get him moving.

Grinning from ear to ear, Danny went to the front. He shook Mr. Bartlett's hand and accepted the First-Place blue ribbon. *I won. I actually won.* He paused for someone to take a picture then wheeled the bike back to his family. He could see the crowd applauding as he went by.

"Congratulations. Excellent job." Dad smiled at his son.

Several people came over to congratulate Danny and admire the bike.

His mom nudged him.

He looked up to see Mr. Bartlett tap the microphone.

Danny looked at his mom.

"I would like to thank you all for coming. Remember to take your entries home. We here at Bartlett's Craft Store would like to remind you about our upcoming sale on all craft items." Mr. Bartlett turned and left the lectern and headed to the front of the store.

"Ready to go home?" Dad signed.

Danny followed, pushing his bike.

Nathan stood by the door, arms crossed.

When Danny reached the boy, he paused, smiled, and rubbed the seat of his bike.

Nathan reached out and tried to grab one of the handlebars.

Danny pulled his bike away. Nothing could spoil the thrill of winning the bicycle of his dreams. Not even Nathan.

The next morning, JoJo and Chloe headed to the park.

Danny tightened his helmet and rubbed an imaginary smudge from the handlebars. Looking around carefully, he jumped on his bike and followed them, keeping his eyes open for Nathan.

The twins were already at the court when Danny, JoJo, and Chloe arrived. They rushed over to admire the bike, while Danny put the lock on.

A game of H-O-R-S-E got underway.

An hour later...

BZZZZZZZZZZZZZ.

Danny pulled the vibrating phone from his pocket.

MOM: Home ... Now ... Party Time

DANNY: Coming.

Danny hopped on his bike, watching for traffic when he crossed the street, and sped home. He needed to do one more thing before his sister got there.

Danny watched from the door of his workshop as JoJo opened the gate, pushing the colorful balloons aside.

Liam, Lili, and Chloe were right behind her.

Danny walked out carrying a box. He put the box on the table and motioned to JoJo.

She ripped off the brown paper to reveal a colorful display case holding her butterflies and white ribbon. She almost knocked Danny over when she gave him a bear hug.

Danny grinned and looked at his parents.

Dad signed, "Perfect."

Mom blew him a kiss.

"Cake and ice cream?" Dad said and signed.

The kids ran to sit at the decorated picnic table.

Danny signed Happy Birthday while everyone sang.

When JoJo blew out all seven candles, Danny raised his hands, twisting his wrists back and forth the way deaf people clap.

Mrs. Tinkham, Liam, Lili, and Chloe followed his example and clapped silently.

JoJo took a bow and signed, "Thank you, thank you."

Mom cut and served the cake while Dad dished up bowls of chocolate ice cream.

JoJo saved the biggest present for last. Inside the box was a clue, which sent her to find another box behind the workshop.

Danny laughed as his sister ran around the yard looking for more boxes and clues until she found a small package taped under the picnic table.

JoJo opened the box. Her eyes grew wide as she took out a bright blue cell phone. "For me?"

Mom and Dad both nodded.

Danny smiled. *Yay. Now she won't pester me to use mine.*

"Yes." JoJo jumped up and down. She held up her phone for everyone to see.

Lucky put his paws on her legs.

JoJo scratched behind the dog's ears. She reached for Danny's arm and showed him the new tags hanging from Lucky's collar. "Look. He's ours."

CHAPTER 13: TEXTING 911

Danny was happy he didn't have to go to the grocery store with his mom, dad, and sister. He enjoyed being alone. He decided to send a picture of his bike to Charlie.

DANNY: I won the bike.

CHARLIE: Wow. Congrats D-Bird.

DANNY: Thanks.

CHARLIE: Any more run-ins with you-know-who?

DANNY: A few times, nothing major.

CHARLIE: If he's like Larry, I bet he's mad you won the bike.

DANNY: Who cares? Gotta work on neighbor's birdhouse now. Catch you later.

CHARLIE: Okay. See ya.

Danny wheeled his bike into his workshop and set the kickstand. He was quite pleased with the cottage design he built for Mrs. Tinkham. *JoJo will love helping me paint this.*

He looked out the window and watched workers tear down the old garage across the alley.

Danny was allowed to take any wood he found in the dumpster. He just had to wait for the workers to leave.

When he saw the men drive off, he walked to the gate and reached for the latch. Danny caught a movement in the alley. Nathan sped toward him on his bike.

Nathan thumbed his nose at Danny and crashed headfirst into the dumpster.

Danny threw the gate open and ran to find Nathan sprawled on the ground, a large red lump forming on his forehead.

Danny pulled out his phone and texted 911.

> **911 OPERATOR:** 911. What is your emergency?

> **DANNY:** Boy on bike hit dumpster. No helmet. Not moving. Hurry.

> **911 OPERATOR:** Do not try to move the boy. Address?

> **DANNY:** 745 Forrest Ave in the alley

> **911 Operator:** Help is on the way.

Danny rubbed Nathan's hand.

Nathan started to stir. He looked up, a tear rolled down his cheek.

Someone reached down and pulled Danny up.

The emergency techs bent over Nathan, checking him out.

"What happened?" One of the EMTs looked at Danny. Danny pulled out his phone.

> **DANNY:** "I'm deaf."

The EMT surprised Danny by signing, "What happened?"

"Ran into dumpster. Not looking."

"Know him?"

Danny signed, "Yes," and fingerspelled Nathan's name then pointed to the last house on the corner.

A police officer went down the alley.

Nathan moved.

The EMT signed, "Boy deaf?"

Danny shook his head. "You sign?"

"Mom deaf."

They looked up to see Mrs. Bartlett running toward them. She grasped her son's hand, tears ran down her face, as they put him on a gurney and into the ambulance.

She turned to Danny. "Thank you." She climbed in the back of the ambulance with Nathan.

The EMT shook Danny's hand and patted him on the back. "Good job. He should be fine. Just needs a doctor to check him out."

Danny watched as the ambulance, lights flashing, went up the alley and turned onto the street. He went back to his workshop and collapsed on the stool, forgetting about the wood in the dumpster. His heart raced and his hands trembled.

He jumped and turned when something touched his shoulder.

His dad leaned on the workbench. "What's wrong?"

Danny took his time and carefully signed what happened.

"You did the right thing, Son. I'm very proud of you."

They walked back to the house together, dad's arm around Danny's shoulder.

Mom flipped the light switch on and off as she entered Danny's bedroom.

He looked up from his computer, eyebrows raised.

"Nathan's mother called. He has a slight concussion and will be in the hospital for a couple of hours. The doctors want to keep an eye on him."

Danny nodded. *Bet he wears a helmet from now on.*

Over the next couple of days, Danny and JoJo worked on Mrs. Tinkham's bright bubble gum pink birdhouse.

Danny gave his sister a "thumbs up" when she painted white daisies around the opening.

After she finished, Danny carried the birdhouse to show their mom and dad who were sitting at the picnic table.

"Very nice. Mrs. Tinkham will love this," Mom said and signed.

Dad smiled. "Pink enough?"

Danny's eyes opened wide when Mrs. Bartlett, Chloe, and Nathan came through the gate. He wondered what was in the large box Mrs. Bartlett carried.

Chloe ran over to JoJo and the two girls sat on the grass, petting Lucky.

Nathan stood near the gate, arms crossed, scowling.

Mrs. Bartlett placed the box on the picnic table and signed. "Thank you." She touched her chin with her fingertips, palm in, and brought her hand out. She motioned to her son.

Danny hid a grin as Nathan shuffled across the yard, hands in his pockets.

He read the boy's lips as Nathan mumbled, "Thank you."

Mrs. Bartlett took the lid off the box and gestured to Danny.

JoJo and Chloe ran over to the picnic table.

Danny looked in the box.

A big, beautiful cake with shiny chocolate frosting nestled inside. Colorful birdhouses decorated the sides.

Written on the top of the cake in bright yellow frosting ...

Danny
Our Hero

ABOUT THE AUTHOR

Jeanne Mansfield has a life-long love of books. While volunteering for Goodwill-Suncoast's Children's Literacy Program, BookWorks, she found a book for children written in Braille. This sparked the idea for *I Talk with My Hands*, a book for both deaf and hearing children. She has written and self-published two toddlers' books. They are interactive, colorful, humorous, and educational. She feels introducing children to books at an early age is vital. Contact Jeanne at jamansfield37@gmail.com.

ABOUT THE AUTHOR

Gail Lenhard is an award-winning author who enjoys writing for all ages and genres. When Jeanne approached her to collaborate on *I Talk with My Hands*, she eagerly agreed, bringing to the project memories of growing up with a deaf mother.

Gail resides in St. Petersburg, Florida, with her husband, daughter, granddaughters, and her many kitties.

Contact Gail at gpl54@yahoo.com

ACKNOWLEDGMENTS

Jeanne:

Gail is not only my co-author, she is my muse, my inspiration, my writing Angel and dear friend. Many acknowledgments begin, "This book would not be possible"... so true.

My wordsmith, my sounding board, and my always-there-for-me-husband, Ed. Much love.

My son Jeff for such a clever book cover and for countless hours of ideas and support. My daughter Janell and son Jay for the many, "What do you think of this" and "Help" texts. My son Johnny for listening and listening.

For Andy Ballestra, neighbor and friend, for his flattering camera.

For Nancy Brett, another neighbor and friend, for giving our manuscript a "fresh eyes" read and a lovely endorsement.

For my very special friend, Naomi Villano for her discerning taste and encouragement. And last but not least our Guardian Angels. Linda Farmer Harris, our Editor *extraordinaire*. Her patience is unlimited. And to Derinda Babcock for her expertise and faith in our book.

Gail:

First, I'd need to acknowledge and thank my co-author and dear friend, Jeanne, who asked me to help write this book in the middle of a pandemic. I have fond memories of sipping hot coffee in the local parks while we worked on the story.

A huge thank you goes out to our wonderful editor, Linda Farmer Harris, for her invaluable guidance. We'd be lost without her.

Likewise, Derinda Babcock who saw the potential our story had and pushed us to succeed.

To Jeff Gilbert for our beautiful book cover.

My family, especially my husband, who endured countless late dinners, endless Zoom meetings, and for listening to me talk about the book over and over.

A huge thank you to my Tampa Word Weavers group for their support and prayers.

And last, but not least, to God. Without him the words wouldn't have come. He is my light and salvation.

REFERENCES/RESOURCES

Adams, Tara: *We Can Sign*. Penguin Group, Inc. (USA). Copyright 2007

Barlow, Rochelle: *101 Easy Signs for Nonverbal Communication: American Sign Language for Kids*. Rockridge Press, Emeryville, CA. Copyright: 2019

Bornstein, Harry & Saulnier, Karen L: *Signing: Signed English: A Basic Guide*. Crown Publishers, Inc. NY. Copyright: 1984

Faunt, Lou: *The American Sign Language Phrase Book*. Contemporary Books, Inc, Chicago, IL Copyright: 1983

Flodin, Mickey: *Signing for Kids*. Rockridge Press, Emeryville, CA. Copyright 2020

The Gallaudet Children's Dictionary of American Sign Language. Gallaudet University Press, Washington, DC. Copyright: 2014

Carson Dellosa Education: *Sign Language 105 Flash Card*s

Pocket Flash Cards for Sign language

WEBSITES:

Signing Savvy: https://www.signingsavvy.com/

Start ASL Course: https://courses.startasl.com/mod/glossary/view.php?id=463

Family Center on Deafness, Largo, FL: https://fcdpinellas.org/

ASL Defined: https://www.asldeafined.com/internal/dictionary-search/?word=learning

Heathline: https://www.healthline.com/health/can-deaf-people-talk

Memphis Oral School for the Deaf: https://mosdkids.org/

Made in United States
Orlando, FL
02 February 2022